Lerner SPORTS

SPORTS ALL-STARS

PETE ALONSO

Jon M. Fishman

Lerner Publications ◆ Minneapolis

Lerner Publications Company
An imprint of Lerner Publishing Group, Inc.
241 First Avenue North
Minneapolis, MN 55401 USA

For reading levels and more information, look up this title at www.lernerbooks.com.

Main body text set in Albany Std 22. Typeface provided by Agfa.

Editor: Rebecca Higgins **Designer:** Mary Ross **Photo Editor:** Todd Strand
Lerner team: Sue Marquis

Library of Congress Cataloging-in-Publication Data

Names: Fishman, Jon M., author.
Title: Pete Alonso / Jon M. Fishman.
Description: Minneapolis, MN : Lerner Publications, [2021] | Series: Sports all-stars (Lerner sports) | Includes bibliographical references and index. | Audience: Ages 7–11 | Audience: Grades 2–3 | Summary: "New York Mets first baseman Pete Alonso literally hit it out of the park during his 2019 MLB debut. The rookie slugger won the Home Run Derby and then led the league in home runs"— Provided by publisher.
Identifiers: LCCN 2020002942 (print) | LCCN 2020002943 (ebook) | ISBN 9781728414744 (library binding) | ISBN 9781728414850 (paperback) | ISBN 9781728414867 (ebook)
Subjects: LCSH: Alonso, Pete, 1994—-Juvenile literature. | Baseball players—United States—Biography—Juvenile literature. | New York Mets (Baseball team)—Juvenile literature.
Classification: LCC GV865.A375 F57 2021 (print) | LCC GV865.A375 (ebook) | DDC 796.357092 [B]—dc23

LC record available at https://lccn.loc.gov/2020002942
LC ebook record available at https://lccn.loc.gov/2020002943

Manufactured in the United States of America
1-48657-49078-3/30/2020

CONTENTS

"ANYTHING'S POSSIBLE"

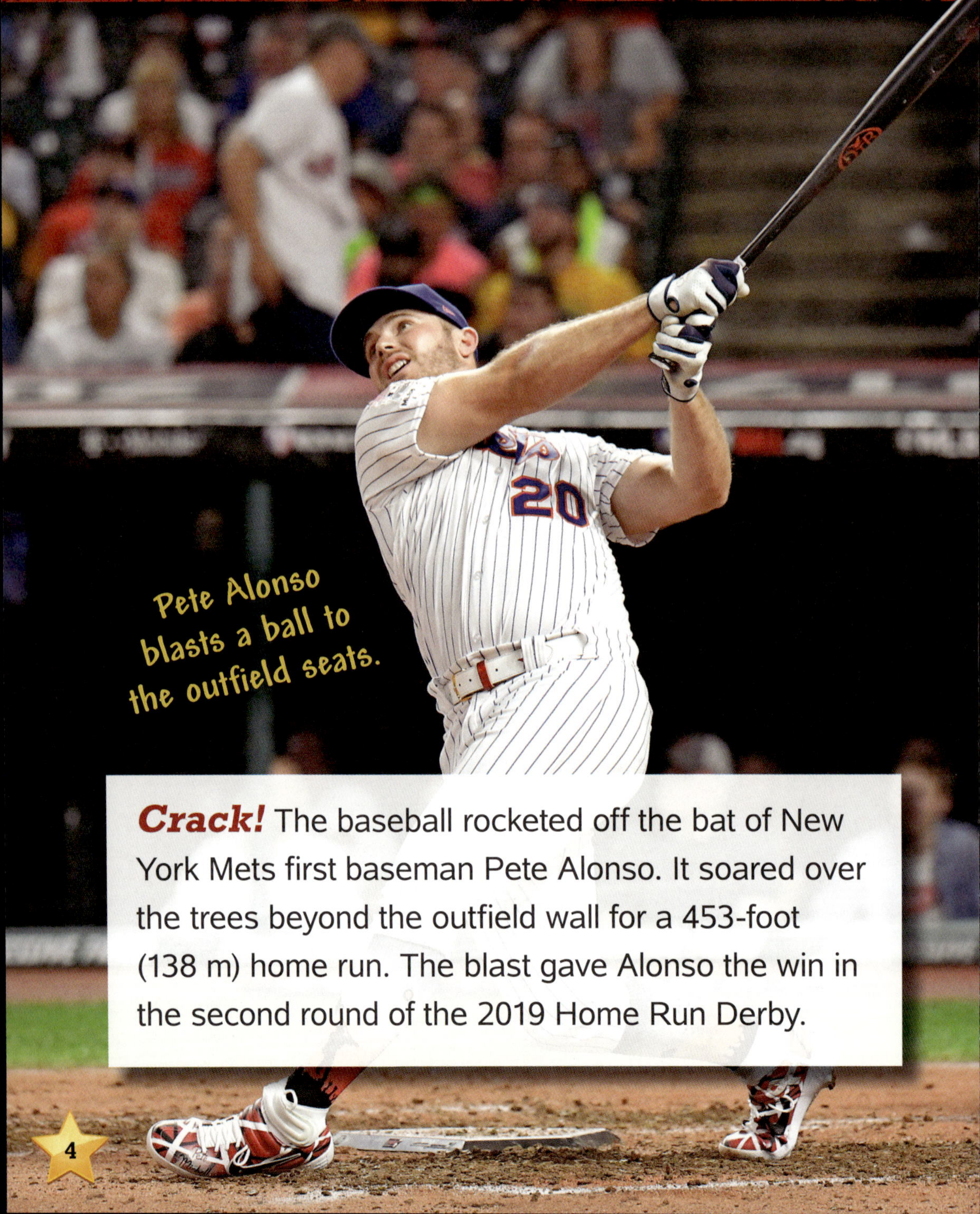

Pete Alonso blasts a ball to the outfield seats.

Crack! The baseball rocketed off the bat of New York Mets first baseman Pete Alonso. It soared over the trees beyond the outfield wall for a 453-foot (138 m) home run. The blast gave Alonso the win in the second round of the 2019 Home Run Derby.

FACTS AT A GLANCE

- **Date of birth:** December 7, 1994
- **Position:** first base
- **League:** Major League Baseball (MLB)
- **Professional highlights:** played his first MLB game in 2019; set the MLB record for home runs by a **rookie** with 53; won the 2019 Rookie of the Year award
- **Personal highlights:** grew up in Tampa, Florida; attended the University of Florida; loves to try new food and places to eat

Next up was the championship round against Vladimir Guerrero Jr. of the Toronto Blue Jays. Guerrero Jr. got off to a slow start before hammering ball after ball over the wall. He finished the round with 22 home runs.

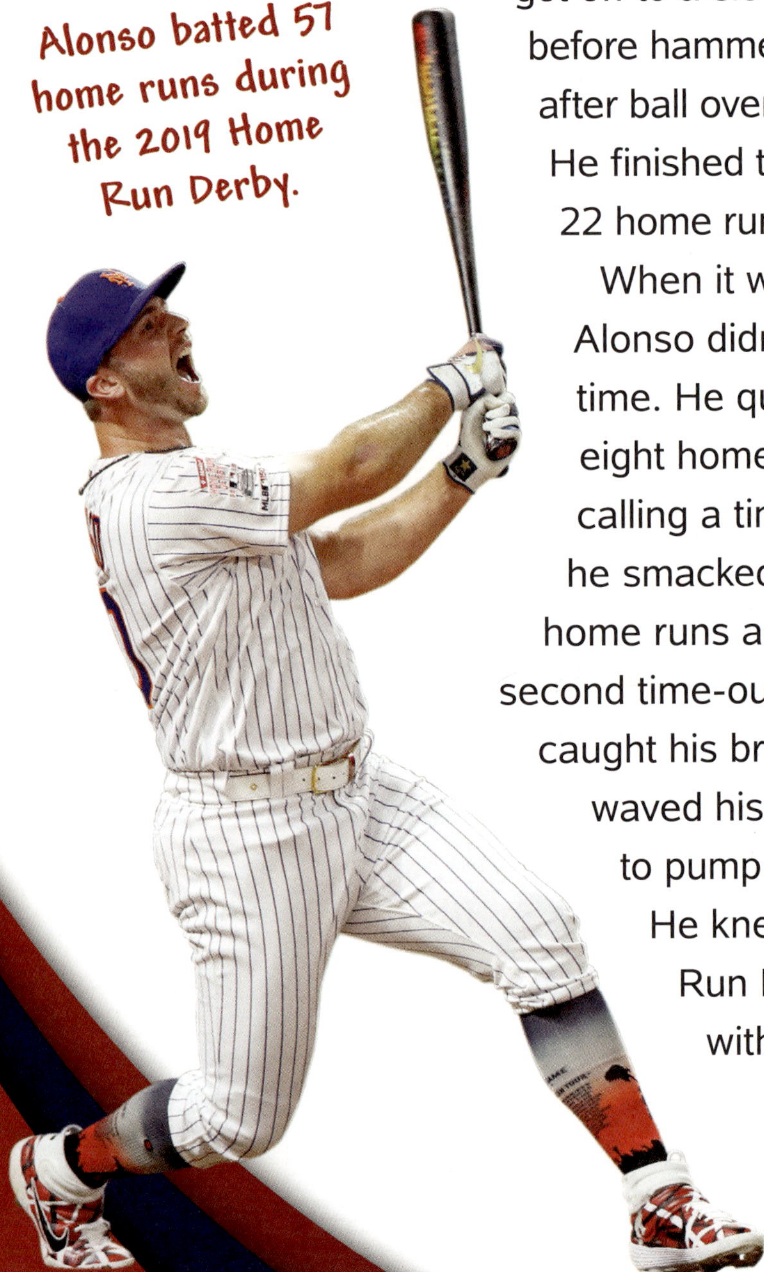

Alonso batted 57 home runs during the 2019 Home Run Derby.

When it was his turn, Alonso didn't waste any time. He quickly clubbed eight home runs before calling a time-out. Then he smacked 10 more home runs and used his second time-out. As he caught his breath, Alonso waved his arms in the air to pump up the crowd. He knew the Home Run Derby title was within reach.

Alonso celebrates winning the 2019 Home Run Derby.

Alonso hit five more home runs to win the championship. He hit 23 homers in the round, including one that soared 459 feet (140 m). As the final blast sailed over the outfield wall, Alonso raised his arms and threw his bat in the air. He hugged his teammates as fireworks exploded in the sky.

Alonso's Home Run Derby victory came midway through his first MLB season. It was a huge win for a rookie. "I've always felt like I can overcome anything," Alonso said. "If I come in with that attitude and keep the fear out, anything's possible."

BASEBALL KID

The Mets play at Citi Field in Queens, New York. But the Alonso family's connection to Queens began long before Alonso started playing baseball there. In the 1930s, his grandfather,

Pete Alonso grew up in Tampa, Florida.

Peter Conrad Alonso, moved to Queens from Spain. Alonso's father, Peter Matthew Alonso, was born in Queens.

Pete was born in Tampa, Florida, on December 7, 1994. Some of his earliest memories are of playing baseball with his dad. At the age of three, he began playing **T-ball**.

Pete wanted to play pro baseball someday. A poster in his room showed the logo of every MLB team. On the poster, Pete wrote, "This is where I want to be."

After T-ball, Pete moved up to Little League baseball. His parents drove him to games all around the Tampa area. They also pitched to Pete so he could practice batting. "I would throw all kinds of balls at him, all sizes," said his mother, Michelle Alonso. "Super Balls, golf balls, water balloons, oranges and grapefruits that fell off the neighbor's trees."

Pete enjoyed other sports too, such as football, soccer, and **lacrosse**. But as a teenager, he decided to give most of his energy to one sport. He chose baseball.

Little League helped prepare Alonso for the major leagues.

At Tampa's Plant High School, Pete proved he made the right choice. He racked up 99 **RBIs** in just 79 career high school games. He also had an amazing .460 **batting average**.

In 2013, Alonso graduated from Plant. That year, pro teams chose more than 1,000 players in the MLB **draft**, including many high school players. But no team chose Alonso.

Instead of starting his pro career, Alonso attended the University of Florida. In 2014, he played first base, third base, and **designated hitter** for the Florida Gators. In his second season, he moved to first base full-time. He batted .301 with five home runs and 32 RBIs.

Alonso was named the 2016 Most Outstanding Player in the region.

Alonso runs the bases after hitting a home run.

The Gators made it to the College World Series, where they lost to the Virginia Cavaliers.

The next season, Alonso was even better. His .374 batting average was the highest Gators average in almost 10 years. He added 60 RBIs to his record and led Florida back to the College World Series. But they lost again, this time to Coastal Carolina University.

In June 2016, Alonso was chosen in the MLB draft. The Mets took him with the 64th overall pick. He would still have to prove himself in the **minor leagues**. But Alonso was one step closer to where he wanted to be.

FROM BROOKLYN TO QUEENS

Alonso hit .286 in 2017 with the St. Lucie Mets.

In 2016, Alonso's pro career began with the Brooklyn Cyclones. For the next three years, he played for several minor-league baseball teams. He practiced his skills, strengthened his body, and worked to become a better player.

Alonso loved to smash the ball, and he swung at every pitch he thought he could hit. But that didn't work as well in the minor leagues as it had in college. Pro pitchers could throw balls that looked hittable, but they sank into the dirt or curved away at the last moment. When that happened, Alonso often swung and missed.

Alonso hits the ball out of the park in 2017.

To stop swinging at so many unhittable pitches, Alonso studied pitchers. His minor-league coaches taught him to look at the angle of a pitcher's throwing arm. He learned to watch how the ball spun

In three minor-league seasons, Alonso batted .290 with 59 home runs and 203 RBIs.

in the air. These clues and others helped Alonso decide quickly if he should swing at a pitch.

In college, Alonso tried different ways to stand at home plate. He held the bat at various angles, raised and lowered his hands, and set his feet in different places. But Alonso's minor-league coaches wanted him to stop moving around so much. That way he wouldn't have to think about how to stand and could focus on batting. The change helped him hit .289 with 18 home runs in 2017.

When Alonso isn't playing baseball, he stays strong with tough workouts. He and a partner warm up with a game of catch before fielding ground balls. He hits the gym, and the real work begins.

To strengthen his legs, Alonso jumps onto a high platform. He steps down and repeats the jump until his

A trainer helps Alonso stretch his legs.

leg muscles burn. Next up is running. He sprints and skips around the gym. Then he grabs heavy weights and works on his arm, chest, and back muscles.

Work in the gym and on the field paid off for Alonso. In 2018, he became one of the top-ranked minor leaguers and showed he was ready for MLB. When the Mets began the 2019 season, Alonso was the team's starting first baseman.

Alonso warms up before a 2019 game.

OFF THE FIELD

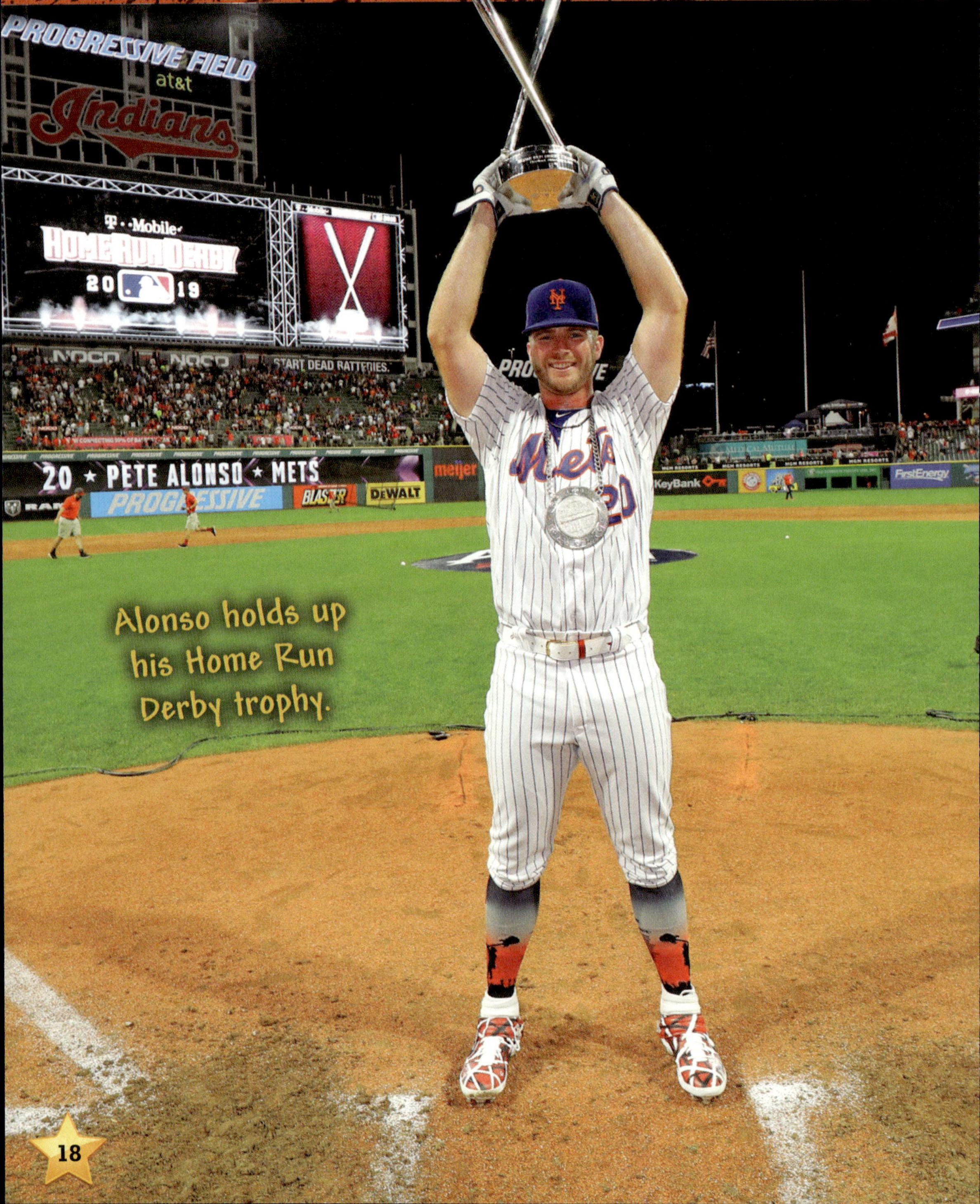

Alonso holds up his Home Run Derby trophy.

Alonso celebrates his derby win with his parents and girlfriend.

With the Mets, Alonso quickly became famous for smashing huge home runs. His victory at the 2019 Home Run Derby came with a $1 million prize. But he didn't keep all the money for himself.

Alonso used some of the prize money to help others. He gave $50,000 to the Stephen Siller Tunnels to Towers Foundation. The group honors military members and **first responders** who lose their lives during duty. He also gave $50,000 to the Wounded Warrior Project to support soldiers recovering from injuries.

The Wounded Warrior Project hosts lunches and other events for veterans.

September 11

On September 11, 2001, planes crashed by terrorists in New York; near Washington, DC; and Pennsylvania killed almost 3,000 people. To honor the victims, Alonso collected the shoe sizes of his Mets teammates. Then he bought special shoes with messages dedicated to the firefighters, police officers, and others who lost their lives. On September 11, 2019, the Mets wore the shoes during a game.

A few weeks later, Alonso gave the shoes to the National September 11 Memorial and Museum. He said he was happy to honor the victims and their families. "You guys will not be forgotten," he said.

A pair of Alonso's shoes on display at the National September 11 Memorial and Museum

Playing for the Mets helps Alonso take part in one of his favorite activities: eating new food. As the team travels around the United States and Canada for games, he visits restaurants in each city. From steak to fish stew, he's willing to try almost anything.

Alonso plays catch before a game in New York. When he's not on the field, he loves to eat out at the city's many restaurants.

Of course, Alonso doesn't have to travel far to find new food. New York is one of the best places in the world for eating out. In 2018, the state had more than 50,000 restaurants, diners, and cafés. About half of those were in New York City, and Alonso loves to explore them.

As a kid, Alonso fished with his grandfather.

Alonso also prepares his own meals at home. "I love to cook," he said. He especially enjoys cooking meat. As a kid, he learned to hunt with his grandfather. Alonso fishes and hunts animals such as elk, deer, and ducks.

RECORD BREAKER

Alonso led the MLB in home runs in the 2019 season.

On August 27, 2019, Alonso made Mets history. Playing against the Chicago Cubs in New York, he hit a long home run to right field. The crowd roared as Alonso ran around the bases. It was his 42nd home run of the year, making him the first Mets player to ever hit that many in a season.

Alonso smiles after hitting his 53rd home run.

Alonso's record-setting smash came with more than a month left to play. He kept hitting home runs, and by September 28, he was ready to break another record. In New York against the Atlanta Braves, he swung and crushed the pitch. The fans jumped to their feet and cheered as the ball flew into the outfield stands.

Alonso cheers with the crowd after breaking the rookie home run record.

It was Alonso's 53rd home run, setting the all-time record for home runs by a rookie. Alonso's teammates streamed onto the field to celebrate with him. As the emotional moment sank in, tears of joy ran down his cheeks.

Alonso was the runaway winner of the 2019 National League Rookie of the Year award. It was an incredible season, but he wants to get even better and win the World Series. "I'm going to use this success, and build off of that as motivation to keep going, keep pushing," Alonso said.

Alonso plans to shatter more records.

Player	Home Runs	Year
Barry Bonds	73	2001
Mark McGwire	70	1998
Sammy Sosa	66	1998
Mark McGwire	65	1999
Sammy Sosa	64	2001
Sammy Sosa	63	1999
Giancarlo Stanton	59	2017
Ryan Howard	58	2006
Luis Gonzalez	57	2001
Hack Wilson	56	1930
Ralph Kiner	54	1949
Pete Alonso	53	2019
George Foster	52	1977
Willie Mays	52	1965

Glossary

batting average: the ratio of a batter's hits per times at bat

designated hitter: a player in the batting order who bats in place of the pitcher

draft: when teams take turns selecting new players

first responders: people such as police officers and firefighters who immediately go to an accident or emergency to help

lacrosse: a game in which players use a long-handled stick with a pouch to catch, carry, and throw the ball

minor leagues: baseball leagues where players train and hope to move up to Major League Baseball

RBIs: runs that are driven in by a batter

rookie: a first-year player

T-ball: baseball in which the ball is batted from a tee rather than being pitched

Source Notes

7 Tyler Kepner, "Pete Alonso's Endless Enthusiasm Leads to Home Run Derby Win," *New York Times*, July 8, 2019, https://www.nytimes.com/2019/07/08/sports/baseball/pete-alonso-home-run-derby.html.

9 Evan Axelbank, "Only 2 Weeks In, Tampa Native Dominating Major Leagues," Fox 13 Tampa Bay, April 16, 2019, https://www.fox13news.com/sports/only-2-weeks-in-tampa-native-dominating-major-leagues.

10 Dean Balsamini, "Mets Star Pete Alonso Credits Mom for His Success," *New York Post*, May 12, 2019, https://nypost.com/2019/05/12/mets-star-pete-alonso-credits-mom-for-his-success/.

21 Associated Press, "Mets' Rookie Pete Alonso Donates 'Never Forget' Cleats to 9/11 Museum," CBS New York, October 1, 2019, https://newyork.cbslocal.com/2019/10/01/pete-alonso-donates-911-cleats/.

23 Kirsten Fleming, "Mets Star Pete Alonso's Secret Passions: Cooking, Hunting and Red Meat," *New York Post*, August 13, 2019, https://nypost.com/2019/08/13/mets-star-pete-alonsos-secret-passions-cooking-hunting-and-red-meat/.

27 Anthony DiComo, "Alonso Runs Away with NL Rookie of the Year," MLB, November 11, 2019, https://www.mlb.com/news/pete-alonso-wins-nl-rookie-of-the-year-award.

Further Information

Home Run Derby
https://www.mlb.com/all-star/home-run-derby

Kelley, K. C. *New York Mets*. Mankato, MN: Child's World, 2019.

MLB
https://www.mlb.com/

Monson, James. *Behind the Scenes Baseball*. Minneapolis: Lerner Publications, 2020.

Savage, Jeff. *Baseball Super Stats*. Minneapolis: Lerner Publications, 2018.

Sports Illustrated Kids—Baseball
https://www.sikids.com/baseball

Index

Photo Acknowledgments

Image credits: Jason Miller/Getty Images, p. 4; Gregory Shamus/Getty Images, p. 6; Alex Trautwig/Major League Baseball/Getty Images, pp. 7, 17, 18, 19, 20; L. M. Kendall/Frederic Lewis/Archive Photos/Getty Images, p. 8; Sean Pavone/Shutterstock.com, p. 9; mTaira/Shutterstock.com, p. 10; Richard Lewis/Corbis/Icon Sportswire/Getty Images, pp. 11, 12; Cliff Welch/Icon Sportswire/Getty Images, pp. 13, 14; Rich Schultz/Getty Images, p. 16; AP Photo/Jake Seiner, p. 21; Mike Stobe/Getty Images, p. 22; Monkey Business Images/Shutterstock.com, p. 23; Jim McIsaac/Getty Images, pp. 24, 25, 26, 27.

Cover: Rich Schultz/Getty Images.